WHAT SPOT?

WHAT SPOT?

by Crosby Bonsall

An I CAN READ Book®

HARPER & ROW, PUBLISHERS

3 3113 02439 6113

WHAT SPOT?
Copyright © 1963 by Crosby Bonsall

LIBRARY OF CONGRESS CATALOG CARD NUMBER: 63–8005
ISBN 0–06–444027–3

First published in 1963. 8th printing, 1976.
First Harper Trophy edition, 1980.

FOR DORIS

Far away in the north,

in the ice and the snow,

by a sea with sailing ships,

a walrus walked.

7

At last he sat down

and looked out to sea,

to the sea with the sailing ships.

8

Then he looked at the snow.

And he looked, and he looked.

For there was a spot in the snow!

9

It was a small black spot.

A small black spot

in the white, white snow.

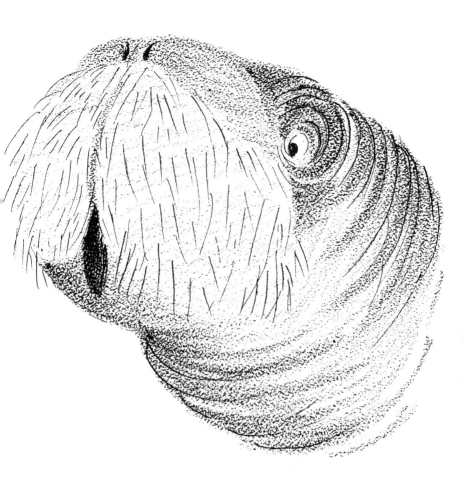

"Now there is a thing,"

the walrus cried.

"There is a thing in the snow.

I wonder what it can be."

11

The walrus began to think.

While he was thinking

a puffin came.

A puffin came and sat down.

"What are you looking at?"

the puffin asked.

"That spot," said the walrus.

"What spot?" asked the puffin.

"*That* spot," said the walrus.

13

"I don't see a spot,"

said the puffin.

"I don't see a spot at all.

I see snow and ice

and sea and sky.

Show me the spot," said the puffin.

"That black spot out there,"

the walrus said.

"Out where?" asked the puffin.

"Out there," said the walrus.

"Oh, *there*," said the puffin.

15

"Yes, there," said the walrus.

"That black spot out there

in the white, white snow."

"Oh, *that* spot," said the puffin.

"Why it's nothing, nothing at all."

"How do you know?" asked the walrus.

"A spot is a spot," said the puffin.

"That's all a spot is. It's a spot."

The walrus was not sure.

"I'm going to see

what that spot is," he said.

"I'm going to see

if that spot's just a spot."

16

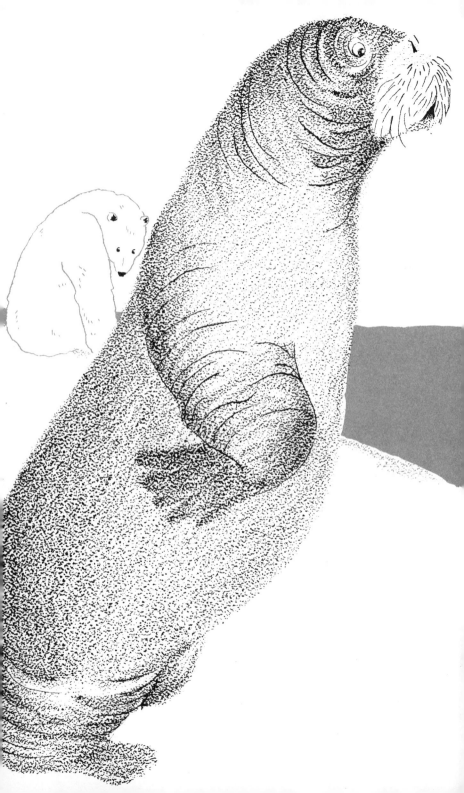

"I told you," said the puffin.

But the walrus did not hear.

And the puffin ran after him.

"I TOLD YOU!" he cried.

"It's nothing, nothing at all."

The spot was not a spot.

The walrus told the puffin so.

"The spot is a thing

deep under the snow

with only its nose sticking out,"

said the walrus.

"It's nothing, nothing at all,"

said the puffin.

The walrus began to dig,

and the puffin looked out to sea.

The walrus dug a little bit,

and the puffin turned to look.

"It's nothing, nothing at all,"

said the puffin, "and that's

not its nose sticking out."

21

The walrus looked.

The puffin looked.

They looked for

a long, long time.

The walrus began to dig some more,

and the puffin looked out to sea.

"It's a sea snake,"
cried the walrus,
"and it's lying here
under the snow."

25

The puffin looked.

The walrus looked.

They looked for a long, long time.

"It's nothing, nothing at all,"

said the puffin.

"Sea snakes swim in the sea.

Sea snakes never swim in the snow."

26

"You are right,"

said the walrus sadly.

He dug some more,

and the puffin looked out to sea.

After a while

the walrus cried, "Hey!"

27

"Hey!" cried the walrus,

"I know what it is.

It's a great big bird.

And it's bigger than you!"

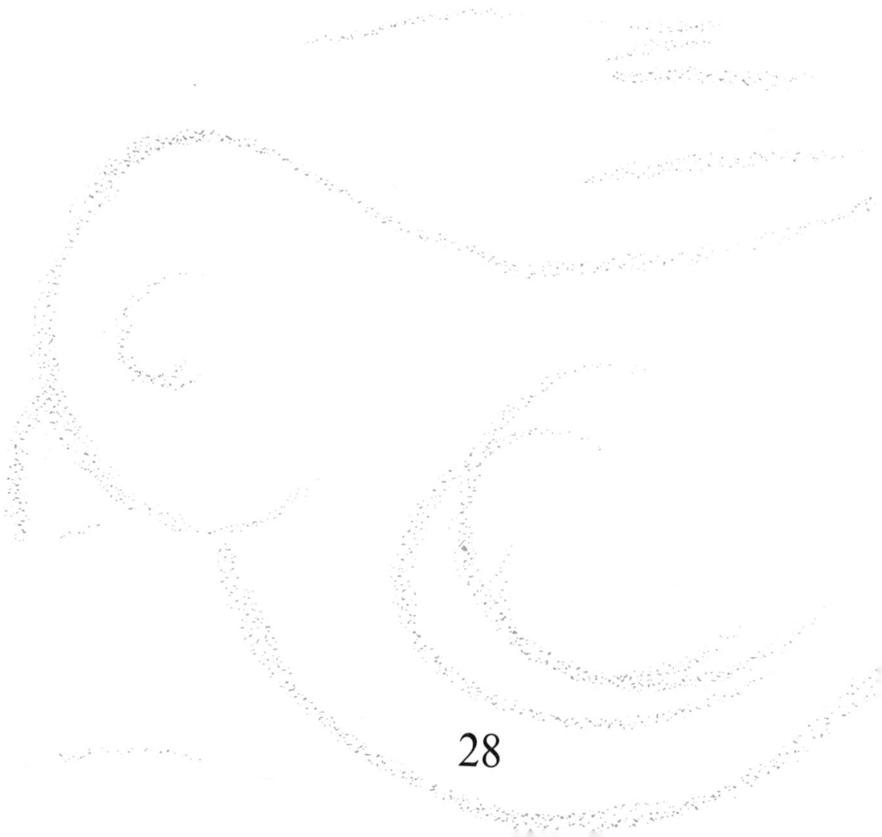

29

The puffin looked.

The walrus looked.

They looked for a long, long time.

"It's nothing, nothing at all,"

said the puffin.

"Birds fly over the snow,

not under the snow."

"You are right,"

said the walrus sadly.

He dug some more,

and the puffin looked out to sea.

After a while the walrus stopped.

"Well," he said, "it has two eyes

and a very long nose.

But I don't know what it is."

The puffin looked.

The walrus looked.

They looked for a long, long time.

"It's nothing, nothing at all,"

said the puffin.

But the walrus dug some more.

"It's snowing," said the walrus.

"I must hurry."

A long time passed.

The walrus dug,

the snow fell,

and the puffin looked out to sea.

The puffin looked out to sea,

the snow fell,

the walrus dug,

and a long time passed.

At last the walrus stopped.

He looked at the thing.

He looked some more.

"I don't know what this is,"

he said.

The puffin looked.

The walrus looked.

They looked for a long, long time.

"It's nothing, nothing at all,"

said the puffin.

"It's something," cried the walrus.

"What can we do with it?"

"Nothing, nothing at all,"

said the puffin.

And he hopped on the thing

to see it better.

40

"I told you it was not a sea snake,"

said the puffin.

"I told you it was not a bird.

There are no eyes.

There is no long nose.

It's nothing, nothing at all."

41

The wind blew hard.

The thing began to roll.

It rolled away from the walrus.

The puffin rolled away with it.

They rolled faster and faster

over the snow.

Faster and faster

over the ice

by the sea with the sailing ships.

The puffin passed a polar bear
who was taking a bath in the sea.
"Help," cried the puffin.
"Don't worry," cried the polar bear,
"it's nothing, nothing at all."

The puffin passed a seal

who was playing with a snowflake.

"Help," cried the puffin.

"Don't worry," cried the seal,

"it's nothing, nothing at all."

The puffin passed a dog

who was rolling snowballs with his nos

"Help," cried the puffin.

"Don't worry," cried the dog,

"it's nothing, nothing at all."

The puffin passed a reindeer

who was dancing in the wind.

"Help!" cried the puffin.

"Don't worry," cried the reindeer,

"it's nothing, nothing at all."

50

The puffin passed a whale

who was resting on a wave.

"Help!" cried the puffin.

"Don't worry," cried the whale,

"it's nothing, nothing at all."

The wind blew the puffin

around and around.

It blew him back to the walrus.

"Help!" cried the puffin.

"I'll help you," cried the walrus.

But it was too late.

There was the hole.

The hole the walrus had dug.

The thing rolled in.

The puffin rolled in.

Snow fell on top of him.

All you could see

was the end of his nose.

The polar bear came out of his bath.

"What are you looking at?"

the polar bear asked.

"That spot," said the walrus.

"What spot?" asked the polar bear.

"*That* spot," said the walrus.

"I don't see a spot,"

said the polar bear.

"That black spot out there,"

said the walrus.

"Out where?" asked the polar bear.

"Out there," said the walrus.

"Oh, there," said the polar bear.

"Yes, there," said the walrus.

"That black spot out there

in the white, white snow

is no spot.

It's a puffin I know."

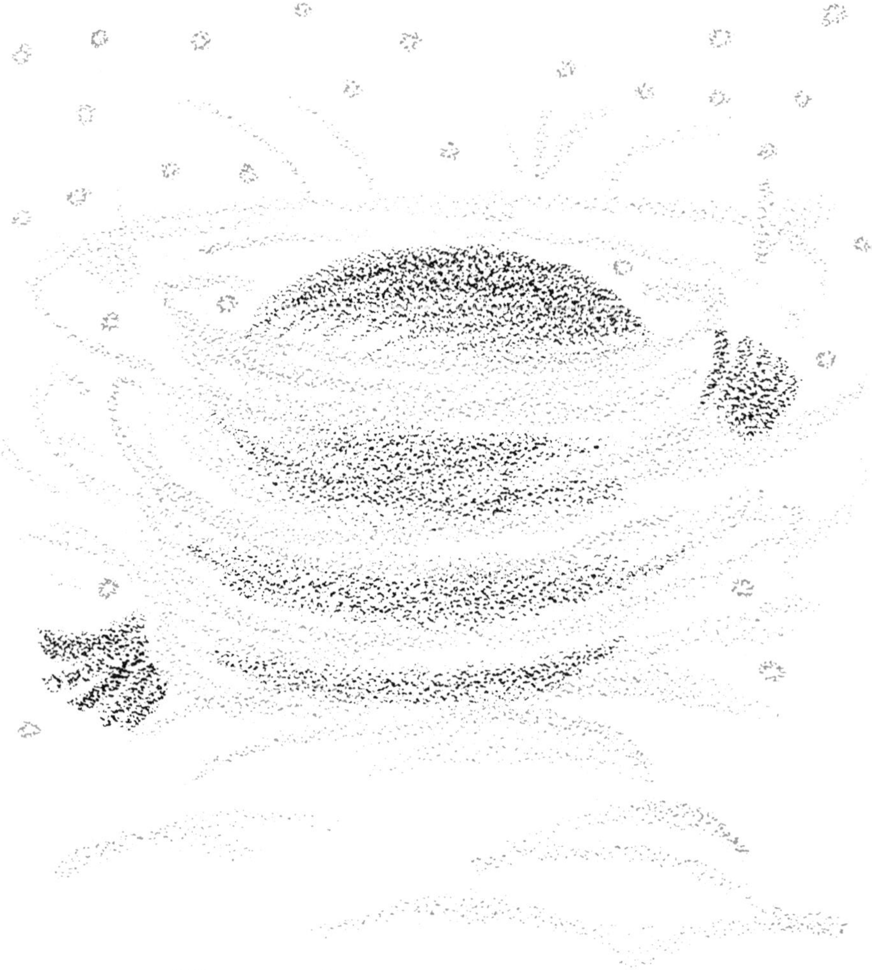

The walrus ran over

and began to dig.

He dug and he dug.

Faster and faster

and FASTER!

There was the puffin

under the snow!

And there was the thing

under the puffin!

The walrus knew what they must do.

And the puffin knew it, too.

"We must do it," said the walrus.

"Yes, we must do it,"

said the puffin.

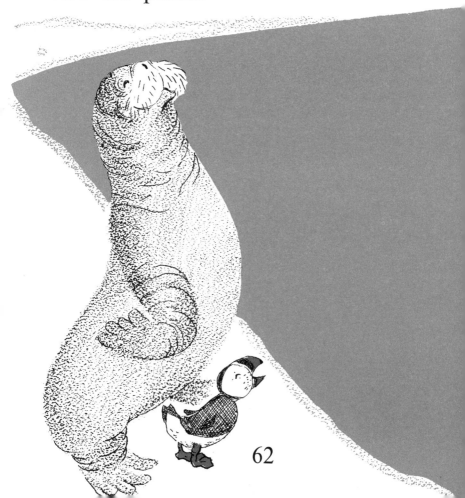

And they did it.

They picked up the thing . . .

and threw it

into the sea!

The walrus and the puffin

sat side by side

and watched the spot

sail out to sea.

The spot grew smaller and smaller

and smaller and smaller

until it was

nothing, nothing at all.